For Ben, my son and now my typographer

First published in Great Britain by HarperCollins*Publishers* Ltd in 2000

1 3 5 7 9 10 8 6 4 2
ISBN: 0 00 198417 9

The HarperCollins website address is:
www.**fire**and**water**.com

Printed in Hong Kong.

DON'T STEP ON THE CRACK!

Colin McNaughton

Collins

An imprint of HarperCollinsPublishers

The story goes that there is a town somewhere and in that town, a street.

On that street is a pavement and on that pavement, a crack.

Whatever you do . . .

Don't
step
on the
crack!

Yes you!

It could
be
any one
of them!

Because
**it's
really
bad
luck!**

But
why
not?

In
what
way?

Well,
for example,
you might fall for
the oldest trick
in the book.

Or you might suddenly
turn into a pig!

You might run into *those* boys.

Or you might turn into your worst nightmare.

Maybe your dad
might decide to
become a hippy.

Or you might notice
something strange about
the new baby.

You might find that your
best friend is not who
you thought he was.

Or your mum
might go for
a younger look.

You might not get
exactly what you want
for your birthday.

Or your new teacher
might not be quite as nice
as your old one.

Your dog might
get you into a bit
of trouble.

Or you might set off
for school one morning
and forget something
really important...

But don't worry!

The crack might not **be** in this pavement!

But then again,
it **might** be!
So just in case…

Don't step on the crack!